LESLEY HOWARTH

Illustrations by Ann Kronheimer

WALKER BOOKS

AND SUBSIDIARIES

LONDON • BOSTON • SYDNEY

For Gramma

First published 1996 by
Walker Books Ltd, 87 Vauxhall Walk
London SE11 5HJ

2 4 6 8 10 9 7 5 3 1

Text © 1996 Lesley Howarth
Illustrations © 1996 Ann Kronheimer

This book has been typeset in Garamond.

Printed in England

British Library Cataloguing in Publication Data
A catalogue record for this book
is available from the British Library.

ISBN 0-7445-4146-8

Class No. __J__   Acc No. __C/69598.__

Author: __HOWARTH, L.__   Loc: __1 1 JUN 1997__

LEABHARLANN
CHONDAE AN CHABHAIN

1. This book may be kept three weeks.
    It is to be returned on / before the last date
    stamped below.
2. A fine of 20p will be charged for every week
    or part of week a book is overdue.

Books by the same author

For older readers

The Flower King

MapHead

The Pits

Weather Eye

CONTENTS

LORD OF THE DARK SETTEE

George was a bit of a dreamer. Sometimes he got so carried away with his thoughts that he muddled things up. If anyone got the wrong end of the stick, it was George. He was famous for it.

One day at school George's
teacher taught the class a new song.
George was dreaming up a story
about spacemen with expanding

10

trousers at the time, so he didn't
catch all the words. It was a funny
song, George thought. It went:

Dance, dance, wherever you may be,
I am the Lord of the Dark Settee.

George thought about the Lord
of the Dark Settee all the way home.
He didn't like the sound of him
much.

When he got home he asked Gramma about it. Gramma was making biscuits.

George stood on a chair and tasted the biscuit mixture. "We sang a song today," he said.

Dance, dance, wherever you may be, I am the Lord of the Dark Settee.

"What does it mean, that song? Only, I don't like him much."

"Who?" Gramma put down her spoon.

"The Lord of the Dark Settee."

"Really, George. You want to clean out your ears."

Gramma laughed when she understood. "The song goes, '*I am the Lord of the Dance, said he.*' There's nothing mysterious about it. And no dark settee."

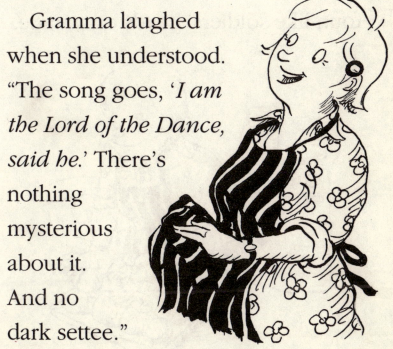

"Oh." George felt relieved. He watched Gramma finish her biscuits. *Dint – dint – dint*. Briskly Gramma pressed down the soft balls of chocolate-coloured dough with a fork. Sixteen fort biscuits, George's favourite. Four rows of four, like soldiers' heads on parade.

Gramma handed George the fork.
"Like to press the last one?"

George licked his lips. Fort
biscuits were biscuits to die for.
He wondered, not for the first time,
how they'd got their name.
It must have been after Fort Biscuit.

Probably they'd baked them there
first, then the recipe had travelled.
By camel, probably, George
thought. Probably over the desert.
Probably—

Pass me those gloves, George. We'd better get these biscuits into the oven.

We better h...

George's face took on a dreamy look. Already the humming oven seemed faint, the sounds of the kitchen far away. We better get them in the oven, George thought, before the men faint of hunger and the fort's attacked by – by *enemies*, what else?

BISCUIT

BANG! WHIZZANG!

The distant sounds of battle filled
the air. The enemy soldiers looked
down from the dunes. Their heads
poked up like coconuts in a row.

George looked around him.
Desert sands stretched away on all
sides, except where the fort blocked
the sun. Quite a small fort, with
dunes and a palm tree beyond.

George slipped in through a grim little door. The door creaked horribly, but the soldier lying on the floor didn't wake up. George stepped over him softly. The soldier wore a strange-looking hat with a flap at the back. He'd written something in the sand, George noticed, before he'd fainted of hunger. Poor Private Hatflap.

SOS BEESKIT.

George crept through passages
and stumbled over steps. A window
showed him the sandy square in
the centre of the fort.

Twenty hungry horses blew
in their empty hayboxes. Twenty
soldiers' washing blew on the

line overhead. Empty barrels labelled GUNPOWDER had rolled onto empty sacks labelled OATMEAL, CORN and BEANS.

Broken buckets and cook-pots, swords and wheels and saddles lay in a muddled pile.

Ladders climbed up to ramparts crowned with cannon and tattered flags. Tin plates and cups and dishes lay piled beside the well. No one had washed up the dishes for a very long time indeed. No one had had any need to.

George climbed up to the ramparts. Soldiers in hats and flaps squinted along their gun barrels. Answering gunsmoke puffed in the sand-dunes. A large and important-looking General covered with medals was giving out orders. No one noticed George at all. The men were up against it.

General Deluge of the French Foreign Legion was thick and dark and strong, like a cup of Legion cocoa. But all the cocoa was gone.

Cookie had only flour. Flour and water were all that was left. The situation was desperate.

George took a deep breath. It was just as he suspected. The fort was surrounded. No food had got through for weeks. The men were down to turnips. They were even eating their boots!

Food was needed urgently, but where – and how – would they get it?

"I tell you ze plan." General Deluge turned to George. "Someone must raid ze enemy camp for food. We need a leettle wriggler no one sees. I seenk you are brave enough to do it?"

George's eyes widened.

Who, me?

"Who, me?"
"No one but you, my leettle cactus. But first, we make ze diversion, yes? Send out Corporal Legume!"

26

Tam-ta-rah-tah, tam-ta-rah-tah-tah!

A trumpet sounded on the signal. The gates opened. Tall and bean-like, Corporal Legume led the attack on the sand-dunes. Ten men rode out behind him.

George and the General watched them go. It was a tense moment for the defenders on the ramparts.

Cookie joined them sorrowfully.
He held up his bowl and spoon.

George peered over the ramparts.
The enemy camels were tethered
beyond the dunes. Their saddlebags
bulged with honey and butter, with
cocoa, spices, vanilla – with every
kind of good thing – and all of it out
of reach. George frowned. It was so
unfair. If they could only reach the
enemy camp, they could cook up a
feast in no time.

"Cocoa!" wailed Cookie. "Vanilla! Sugar! Butter! You wriggle over ze sand for us, yes? You fetch ze beeskit-makings now?"

"Corporal Legume makes good diversion, yes?" The General looked at George. "Now for leetle wrigglers. Wrigglers no one sees."

George opened his mouth to say, I don't think so! But someone was

pulling at his trousers – someone he'd only seen once in his life, on the floor in the room downstairs.

"Beeskits!" croaked poor Private Hatflap. "We are starving! Ze end of the road, we are reaching it! Ze bottom of the barrel, we are scraping it! We cannot go on! Cocoa! Beeskits! *Now!* Weezout zem ze fort – it will fall!"

THE WRIGGLER

George licked his lips. Cocoa.
Biscuits. *Now.* He slipped down the
steps to the guardroom. He opened
the guardroom door. The dunes
looked a long way off. How good a
wriggler *was* he? Could he reach the
enemy camp and bring home the
biscuit ingredients?

Suddenly George decided. If he
didn't try, who would? *Biscuits ho!*
Could he save the fort?

George wriggled as he'd never wriggled before in his life. His elbows burned. His knees ached. Hot, stinging sand blew into his face, but still he wriggled on. The sun blazed. Smoke billowed down from the sand-dunes.

No one noticed George until he reached the camels.

"Stop! 'alt!" The camel keeper shouted.

George jumped up.

Nothing would stop him now.

"Right," said George. "The thing
is, we're rather hungry."

"I am hungry too," Salif said. "The
camels, they have many good
things on their backs. But Salif has
no way to cook them."

35

The camels stirred. George sized them up. A line of camels crossing the desert nose-to-tail was sometimes called a caravan, George remembered. But until now he'd never known why. The largest camel *did* look a bit like a caravan. It was as long as his Uncle Jim's caravan, George thought, and probably almost as wide. Plus it was piled with pots and pans and nets of nuts and honey-crocks, with swinging strings of onions and bulging sacks of flour and beans and darkest Arabian coffee.

"There's no time to guess," said George. "Do a dare."

"OK." Salif grinned. "I dare you – wriggle through Tomba's legs. Not touch Tomba *at all*, then I tell you whatever you want."

"And Tomba is...?"

"My king of all camels. My so-big-he-shades-the-sun camel."

The caravan! George looked at Tomba. Tomba had feet like sink-plungers. He was cross-eyed and smelly and he spat. With all his backpacks, he probably weighed about a tonne.

A cannonball flew over the ridge.
The fort had been under fire too
long. It couldn't hold out much
longer.

If wriggling through a camel's
legs was what it took to save the
fort, he would have to do it. If only,
George thought, it wasn't the
biggest camel of all.

BISCUITS HO!

Tomba the camel swayed
dangerously. His sink-plunger feet
stood on either side of George's
head. George closed his eyes and
rocked from side to side.

Tomba batted his ears and tail.
He belched and blew and hiccuped.
But he didn't move his feet at all.

Slowly, George inched between
them. Slowly, quietly, he wriggled
into the shadow of Tomba's belly –
and slowly he wriggled out on the
other side.

Last of all he drew out his legs,
careful not to touch a single hair.
It was over! Tomba hadn't moved
or crushed him, and he'd done it!

George jumped up with a shout.
"Cocoa! Which camel? *Well?*"

Salif seized Tomba's halter and
handed it to George.

Tomba has cocoa.
You want him, we go!

They jumped up and rode like
the wind. Nothing much stopped
Tomba. On the way they met

Corporal Legume and swung him up
behind them. They rode over the
dunes, across the sand, with cries of …

… and in through the gates at a
gallop. Into Cookie's kitchen with
the cry of, "Fire up your ovens!
Butter! Cocoa! Vanilla! Sugar!
Biscuits ho!"

Soon the word spread like
wildfire. All over Fort Biscuit men
threw up their hats for joy. Private
Hatflap wrung his hands.

In no time Cookie's mixing bowl was busy. In went butter, sugar, vanilla. In went flour and cocoa. Cookie rolled the mixture into balls. George pressed the balls down with a fork. Cookie posted them quickly into red-hot ovens. Soon the smell of biscuits was wafting through the fort.

"We had better get zese beeskits out of ze oven," Cookie said after a while. "Feefteen minutes is too much cooking already. I seenk you take up ze first plate?"

George climbed the stairs to the
ramparts with a stack of delicious
biscuits. Weak cheers greeted him.
Gladly, the men gathered round.
They each helped themselves to a
biscuit – then another, and another.
For a long time there was silence.

Then Private Hatflap jumped up.

George went
down to the
kitchen for more.
He climbed to the
ramparts with another
tray of hot chocolatey
biscuits. The men fell on
them greedily. George went
back to the kitchen; up to the
hungry men, back to
the steaming
ovens. At last
the General
himself
took down
the very last
tray.

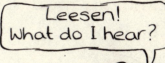

A trumpet sounded overhead.

"Ze men, zey are rallying!" cried General Deluge. "Ze enemy, zey are retreating! Ze fort, she is saved by a beeskit! Bravo, my brave Georgie boy – "

"That's Lord George to you," put in George modestly. "Of Arabia."

"My Lord Meester Georgie of Arabia," finished General Deluge. "Ze keys of Fort Biscuit are yours! I award you ze Medal of Honour!"

GEORGE OF ARABIA

"We'd better get these biscuits out," said Gramma. "Fifteen minutes is plenty. Probably too much."

"That's what Cookie said," said George.

"Cookie?" Gramma lifted the biscuits out of the oven. "When did Cookie say that?"

"When we saved the fort."

"When did you save the fort?"

"When we cooked the fort biscuits, of course."

"*Fork* biscuits," corrected Gramma. "We pressed them down with a *fork*. That's why they're called—"

FORK biscuits.

"*Fort* biscuits," George said firmly. "Because they saved the fort."

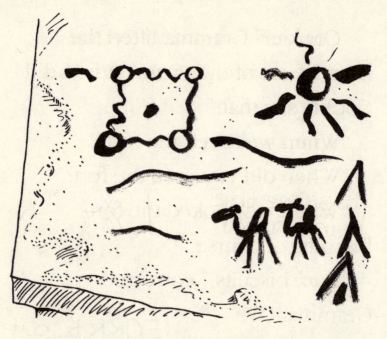

George drew the fort in the flour on the table. He put in the well in the middle, the sand-dunes, the camels, the enemy camp. Hadn't he wriggled when no one else could? Hadn't he dared Salif's dare and brought back the cocoa? Helped to feed the men and save the day?

Gramma listened as George told
her the story of Fort Biscuit. That
was the best thing about her.
Gramma *always* listened.

Gramma scooped the biscuits
onto a tray. She handed George the
sieve. "Want to dust them with
sugar?"

George dusted the biscuits. "Good ones, aren't they?" he said.

Gramma nodded. "So how *did* they save the fort?"

"Easy," George said. "Try one and see."

Gramma took one.

George closed his eyes. Warm cocoa biscuit melted blissfully inside his mouth. He opened his eyes again slowly.

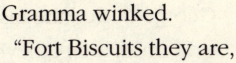

Gramma winked.

"Fort Biscuits they are, from now on. I think they'd save *any* fort, don't you?"

"They saved Fort Biscuit," George said, "and it was *me* who helped."

"You are funny, George," Gramma laughed. "I hope you *never* clean out your ears."

George grinned. "Me too."

Some mistakes were worth their weight in – cocoa!

FORT BISCUITS

180g butter or margarine
60g icing sugar
120g plain flour
60g cornflour
30g cocoa powder
1/2 teaspoon vanilla essence

Preheat oven to gas mark 5 or 375°F. Cream butter and sugar together. Add flour, cornflour and cocoa powder. Add vanilla essence. Knead into a soft dough. Roll dough into walnut-sized balls. Place on baking tray and press down once with a wet fork, so not too thin. Bake for 12 to 15 minutes. Dust with more icing sugar when cool.

FORT BISCUITS